# Ally the Dolphin Fairy

To Alexandra Mair Spinochia,
a very special friend of the fairies!

Special thanks
to Sue Mongredien

No part of this work may be reproduced, stored in a retrieval
system, or transmitted in any form or by any means, electronic,
mechanical, photocopying, recording, or otherwise, without written
permission of the publisher. For information regarding permission,
write to Rainbow Magic Limited c/o HIT Entertainment,
830 South Greenville Avenue, Allen, TX 75002-3320.

ISBN 978-0-545-27035-9

All rights reserved. Published by Scholastic Inc., 557 Broadway,
New York, NY 10012, by arrangement with Rainbow Magic Limited.

SCHOLASTIC, LITTLE APPLE, and associated logos are trademarks
and/or registered trademarks of Scholastic Inc. RAINBOW MAGIC
is a trademark of Rainbow Magic Limited. Reg. U.S. Patent &
Trademark Office and other countries. HIT and the HIT logo are
trademarks of HIT Entertainment Limited.

12 11 10                                    14 15 16/0

Printed in the U.S.A.                        40

This edition first printing, March 2011

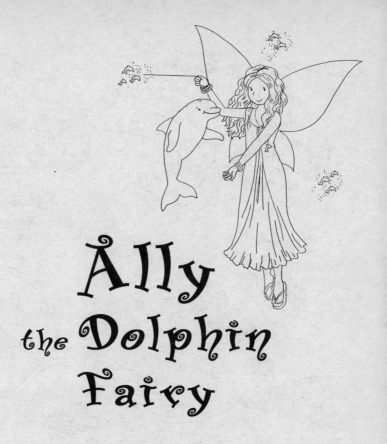

# Ally
## the Dolphin
## Fairy

by Daisy Meadows

SCHOLASTIC INC.

New York   Toronto   London   Auckland
Sydney   Mexico City   New Delhi   Hong Kong

With the magic conch shell at my side,
I'll rule the oceans far and wide!
But my foolish goblins have shattered the shell,
So now I cast my icy spell.

Seven shell fragments, be gone, I say,
To the human world to hide away,
Now the shell is gone, it's plain to see,
The oceans will never have harmony!

# Contents

## Off to Fairyland

Kirsty Tate and Rachel Walker stepped off the bus and blinked in the sunshine. The two girls were staying with Kirsty's gran in Leamouth for spring vacation. Today they'd come to Lea-on-Sea, a small seaside resort along the coast.

"I've got some shopping to do, so I'll meet you back here at noon," Kirsty's gran said, getting off the bus. "Have fun!"

"We will," Kirsty assured her. "See you later, Gran." Then she turned to Rachel. "Come on, let's go down to the beach!"

It took the girls only a few minutes to walk down the sandy steps to the curving bay. The beach was packed with families enjoying the sun. The sky was a clear, fresh blue, and a breeze ruffled the tops of the waves. Lots of children were swimming. Above them, shrieking sea gulls soared, stretching their strong white wings.

"This is great!" Rachel said, slipping off her shoes and wiggling her bare toes in the warm sand. She pointed to the far edge of the bay. "Do you want to go over there? It's a little less crowded."

The girls made their way across the beach, snaking between lounge chairs and sandcastles. Then Kirsty stopped suddenly and bent down. "Hey, look at this shell," she said, picking it up to show Rachel. "It's really sparkly."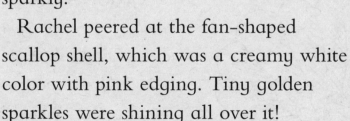

Rachel peered at the fan-shaped scallop shell, which was a creamy white color with pink edging. Tiny golden sparkles were shining all over it!

Rachel's heart beat faster with excitement as she looked at Kirsty. "That looks like fairy magic," she whispered.

"Just what I was thinking," Kirsty replied, smiling. "Oh! I can feel something underneath it, too."

She flipped the shell over in her palm and both girls saw a tiny gold scroll tucked into it, tied with a pretty red ribbon. Rachel untied the ribbon and unfurled the scroll. Then both girls leaned over to read the tiny writing.

*"King Oberon and Queen Titania hereby invite you to the Fairyland Ocean Gala,"* Kirsty read in a whisper. "Wow!" Rachel felt a rush of

excitement. She and Kirsty had been
to Fairyland many times now. They
had enjoyed lots of wonderful fairy
adventures, but the thought of visiting
their fairy friends was always thrilling.
"What are we waiting for?" she said.
"Let's hide behind these rocks so nobody
sees us travel to Fairyland!"

Once they were hidden from view,
Rachel and Kirsty opened the pretty
golden lockets they were wearing.
The lockets had been a present from
the fairy king and queen. They
contained magical fairy dust that could
transport the girls to Fairyland. Their
fingers trembling with excitement, the
two friends each took a pinch of the
sparkling pink dust and sprinkled
themselves with it.

Instantly, a glittering whirlwind spun
up around them, and they felt themselves
shrinking smaller and smaller. Soon they
were fairy-size. Kirsty just managed
to grab Rachel's hand as they spun
around very quickly. Then, after a few
moments, the whirlwind slowed and the
girls felt themselves lowered gently to the
ground.

"Another beach!" Rachel exclaimed
in delight, gazing around. "A Fairyland
beach!"

"And we're fairies!" Kirsty cried,
fluttering the beautiful gauzy wings
on her back. She loved the way they
shimmered in the sunlight with all the
colors of the rainbow.

The two friends were standing on
the beach next to the Fairyland Royal

Aquarium, an unusual building made of glass and stone. The king and queen's gala was in full swing. Hundreds of fairies were dancing to lively music, competing in swimming races, enjoying boat rides, and eating the most wonderful-looking ice cream. "There are the Party Fairies," Kirsty said, spotting their old friends flying around, making sure that everyone was having fun. "Oh, and there's Shannon the Ocean Fairy!"

Rachel and Kirsty had met Shannon during a very special summer adventure the last time they'd had a vacation in Leamouth. Shannon was fluttering toward them now, followed by some other fairies the girls didn't recognize.

"Hello, Kirsty! Hello, Rachel!" Shannon cried happily. "It's great to see you again. These are my Ocean Fairy helpers. They take care of the creatures in the Royal Aquarium and throughout all the oceans in the human world, too!"

Shannon introduced the fairies: Ally the Dolphin Fairy, Amelie the Seal Fairy, Pia the Penguin Fairy, Tess the Sea Turtle Fairy, Stephanie the Starfish Fairy, Whitney the Whale Fairy, and Courtney the Clownfish Fairy.

"Hi," said Whitney, who was wearing

a brightly patterned dress. "Have
you been to one of our ocean parties
before?"

"No," Kirsty replied. "But this
one looks great! Are you celebrating
something special?"

"We hold a gala like this every
summer," explained Tess, who had her
blond hair in two long braids. "It's lots of
fun, but important, too. Shannon plays

a song on the golden conch shell that ensures peace and harmony throughout the ocean for the whole year. It's up there, see?"

Tess pointed at a small stage in front of the aquarium. A table stood in the middle, covered in a midnight-blue velvet cloth. On top of the cloth sat a large golden shell, glittering with magic.

"Speaking of which, it's about time I got started," said Shannon. She winked at Rachel and Kirsty. "Wish me luck!"

As Shannon walked onstage, a hush fell over the party. "Good afternoon, everyone," Shannon said in her tinkling voice. "I hope you're all having a fantastic time at our annual Ocean Gala."

"No!" came an angry voice. "No, I

am *not* having a good time, at all!"

Rachel's mouth fell open in shock as a grumpy-looking figure barged through the crowd and onto the stage. "Jack Frost!" she whispered. "What's he doing here?"

Kirsty bit her lip. Jack Frost was such an awful troublemaker! "I don't know," she replied, "but it looks like we're about to find out."

## Shattered!

"Excuse me . . ." Shannon said politely, but Jack Frost grabbed the microphone and began addressing the crowd.

"I hate the ocean!" he ranted. "I can't swim, and I don't like getting sand between my toes. It's no fun for me, so I don't see why I should let any of you enjoy yourselves. Goblins, get to work!" he ordered.

At his words, a group of five goblins rushed onstage and grabbed the golden conch shell. They ran off with it before Shannon or any of the other Ocean  Fairies could stop them. In true goblin style, they immediately began arguing about which way to go and who was going to carry it. The goblins pulled the shell back and forth between them. Suddenly, it flew high into the air—and smashed to the ground, breaking into several pieces.

Shannon ran over to collect the shards of broken shell, but Jack Frost was too fast for her.

"*The shell may be shattered, but I don't care. I'll scatter its pieces everywhere!*" he chanted, waving his wand at the fragments of shell. A blast of icy magic burst from his wand, spiraling and whirling around the seven broken pieces. They went flying into the air, and then, with a puff of smoke, they were gone. "Your precious shell is scattered all over the human world now!" Jack Frost sneered.

"You'll never find the pieces, and your ocean world will be in chaos—forever!" With another wave of his wand and a horrible cackle of laughter, he and his goblins vanished from sight.

Shannon turned very pale. "This is awful," she said anxiously. "Until I 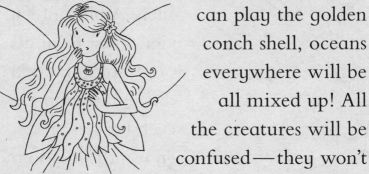 can play the golden conch shell, oceans everywhere will be all mixed up! All the creatures will be confused—they won't be able to find their homes or families. What are we going to do?"

Queen Titania stepped onto the stage and put a comforting arm around Shannon. "Don't worry," she said. "I can't stop Jack Frost's spell, but I'll do my best to change it. Come, let's go to the Royal Aquarium, and I'll explain my plan. Ocean Fairies, you should come, too," she said. Then her eyes fell on Kirsty and Rachel, and her serious expression softened. "Hello, my dears," she added. "Would you join us as well? We need your help again."

Kirsty and Rachel both curtsied. "Of course," Kirsty said politely.

They followed the queen into the huge entrance hall of the Royal Aquarium. It had a polished marble floor, and lots of glass tanks arranged along one side. The stained glass windows at the top of the hall featured pictures of different sea creatures: mighty whales, leaping dolphins, dainty seahorses, and many more. Sunlight streamed through the windows, casting colorful reflections onto the floor.

The glass tanks varied in size, and each housed a single creature: a dolphin, a seal, a penguin, a starfish, a turtle, a whale, and a clownfish. Kirsty noticed that all seven creatures were surrounded by faint golden sparkles.

"This is my plan," Queen Titania announced. "These are the seven

magic ocean creatures who belong to
our Ocean Fairies. I now proclaim
them the guardians of the seven pieces
of the golden conch shell." She waved
her wand, and a jet of silver magic burst
from its tip and swirled around the
aquarium. The light from the magic

was so bright, Rachel had to shut her
eyes. When she opened them again, the
tanks were empty. The magic ocean
creatures had disappeared!

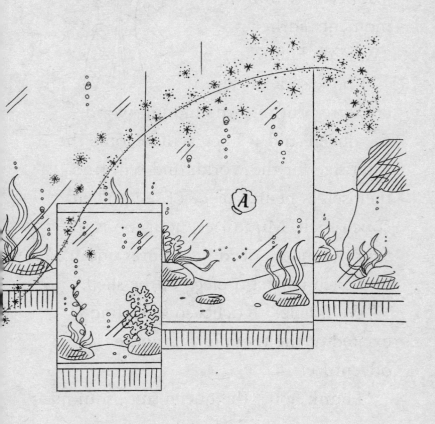

"Where did they go?" Ally gasped, peering at the tank where her dolphin had just been swimming moments earlier. "Where's Echo?"

"I have sent all seven creatures out into the human world," the queen said. "They will become the right size for the world, and will find themselves near a piece of the golden conch shell. My fairies, your job is to find the magic ocean creatures again, and each collect a piece of the shell."

"We'll help," Rachel said, feeling excited at the thought of another fairy adventure.

"Thank you," the queen said, smiling

at Rachel and Kirsty. Then she turned to Ally. "I will send you out first," she declared. "Kirsty and Rachel will help you look for Echo. Good luck!"

She pointed her wand first at Ally, then at the two girls. A glittering whirlwind immediately lifted them off their feet and into the air.

# Where's Echo?

creatures
er tunnels
stadium.

When Kirsty and Rachel landed, they
were back to their normal sizes, and
were standing outside a building called
Ocean World. "It's a sealife center,"
Kirsty realized, reading a nearby
poster. "This says *See ocean creatures in our
amazing underwater tunnels and our unique
oceanside stadium.* Perfect!"

"Echo must be inside somewhere," Ally said, hovering near Rachel's shoulder. She looked almost like a glittering butterfly, with her beautiful long, lavender dress and sparkly wings, Kirsty thought.

"Come on, girls, let's go in," the fairy said.

Kirsty's grandma had given the girls some spending money, so luckily they had just enough to pay the entrance fee. As they went in, Ally tucked herself into Rachel's pocket so that she'd be out of sight. They walked through the aquarium, and couldn't help but notice that the ocean creatures were acting very strange.

"Look," Rachel said in surprise, stopping in front of

one glass tank filled with tropical fish.
"These angelfish are doing somersaults!"

Kirsty stared. Sure enough, the pretty
striped fish were swimming around and
around in the water. They looked very
dizzy!

Farther along, the girls saw three
catfish in a tank who were tickling each
other with their whiskers. In the next
tank, some octopuses had gotten their

tentacles all tangled together in knots.

"This is awful," Ally said, looking worried. "And it's all because Shannon didn't get to play her song on the golden conch shell. We've got to find the pieces to put the shell together again as soon as possible."

Just then, an announcement came over the loudspeaker. "Ladies and gentlemen, our wonderful Wild Dolphin Show is about to begin. Please take your seats in the oceanside stadium!"

"Dolphins?" Kirsty said excitedly. "Echo might be there. Come on!"

The girls and Ally quickly made their way to the oceanside stadium. It was an open-air arena with a wonderful view right down to the sea. A wooden jetty had been built close to the water, and

Rachel and Kirsty could see some boys in Ocean World uniforms there, carrying buckets of fish.

Two dolphin trainers strode onto the jetty and waved at the audience. "Hi, everyone!" one of them called. She had a blond ponytail and a big smile. "Welcome to the Ocean World Wild Dolphin Show. You're about to see dolphins performing some amazing tricks."

"These dolphins are wild dolphins. They live freely in the ocean," said the second trainer, a man with short brown hair. "But they love showing what they can do—and they love their dinner, too!" He grinned and threw a handful of fish into the sea. Immediately, a

group of dolphins appeared, swimming gracefully in and out of the water.

"I love how they look like they're smiling," Rachel said, her eyes glued to the beautiful creatures.

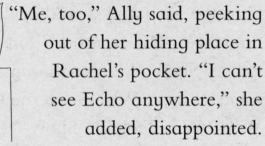

"Me, too," Ally said, peeking out of her hiding place in Rachel's pocket. "I can't see Echo anywhere," she added, disappointed.

"For our first trick, the dolphins are going to jump through this hoop," the first trainer announced, showing the audience a bright red hoop. "They love doing this—just watch!" She held the hoop out above the water . . . but the dolphins didn't seem interested. In fact, they completely ignored the trainer and her hoop.

The trainer frowned and looked
embarrassed. "Hey, guys," she coaxed
the dolphins, waving the hoop around.
"Over here!"

Ally shook her head. "Oh, no," she
whispered. "This is because the golden
conch shell is missing, I know it. The
dolphins have forgotten what to do."

It soon became clear that the dolphins didn't want to jump through the hoop, or balance beach balls on their noses, or do any tricks at all. "I'm really sorry, everybody," the man with brown hair said, "but we'll have to cancel today's show. I don't know what's wrong with the dolphins. Usually, they love performing!"

A sigh of disappointment went up from the audience and people got to their feet to leave. Rachel stood up, too, but Kirsty grabbed her hand to stop her. "Wait," she said. "Look at those boys."

Rachel and Ally peered down to see what Kirsty had noticed. The two boys who'd been carrying buckets of fish earlier were messing around on the jetty now, throwing fish at each other. One

boy's hat fell off. The girls and Ally gasped as they saw what a pointy nose the boy had . . . and what green skin, too!

"They're goblins!" Rachel yelped, her stomach lurching at the sight. What were they doing here?

"Oh, no!" Ally cried. "Jack Frost must have realized that Queen Titania changed the spell. He sent his goblins into the human world to find the missing shell pieces before we do!"

## Goblins Underwater

The three friends fell silent. This was terrible! They couldn't let the goblins find the missing shell pieces first. But then Ally spoke again, and this time she sounded much more cheerful. "Look, there's Echo! Do you see that sweet little dolphin following the others?"

Rachel and Kirsty looked down at
the sea. The group of dolphins was
heading away from the stadium, and
behind them swam a small, pretty
dolphin, whose silvery skin sparkled in
the sunlight. "The piece of shell must be
somewhere nearby," Kirsty announced.
"We've got to get in the water and go
after Echo."

Ally smiled and a dimple flashed in
her cheek. "No sooner said than done,"
she said. Ally waved her wand, and
silver sparkly fairy dust flowed around
Kirsty and Rachel, turning them into

fairies again. "Now you each need one
of these," she said, waving her wand
again to create two magic bubbles. The
bubbles settled over the girls' heads like
scuba diving helmets, then disappeared
with a *pop*. Rachel and Kirsty knew
from their adventures with Shannon
that they would now be able to breathe
underwater. They would stay warm and
dry, too!

"Ready? Let's go!" said Ally. Then the
three of them flew over to the sea
and plunged into the water.
They started swimming after
Echo and the other dolphins.
Rachel flashed a huge
smile at Kirsty as
they swam
through the

cool, clear water. What an adventure
this was turning out to be!

The three fairies followed the dolphins
deep into the ocean, all the way to a
beautiful underwater grotto. It was full
of colorful sea anemones and waving
fronds of seaweed. Ally gave a high
whistle, and Echo turned her head.

At the sight of her fairy friend, Echo made a happy clicking sound and swam over right away, looking delighted. Ally gave Echo a hug and stroked her silvery nose. "Hello there," she said, smiling. "Have you seen a piece of the golden conch shell anywhere?"

Echo made more clicking sounds.

Ally interpreted Echo's clicks. "She's asked the other dolphins, but they haven't seen anything either. She hasn't searched this grotto yet, though. Maybe we can do that together."

The friends swam farther into the cave and began looking all over for a piece of the golden conch shell. "There's something shimmering down there," Kirsty said excitedly, pointing at one corner of the cave floor. "I wonder if it might be the shell?"

But just as they were about to go and take a closer look, Ally whispered a warning. "There are divers heading this way," she said. "Hide!"

She, Kirsty, and Rachel immediately darted behind a large clump of seaweed so that the divers wouldn't see them. The girls knew that the fairies had to be kept a closely guarded secret from other humans.

The two divers swam closer. The light was dim this far down in the ocean, but

Rachel couldn't help noticing that these
divers had very big feet. So big, in fact,
that they had no need for flippers. Then
she noticed that the divers' skin looked
rather greenish, too. . . .

She elbowed Kirsty. "They're goblins!"
she whispered. "And I think they see the
shell!"

# A Sparkling Shell

Rachel was right. The divers were goblins! Even worse, they were heading straight for the sparkling piece of shell that lay in the corner of the cave.

"Quick!" Kirsty cried. "We've got to get there first!"

The three fairies and Echo swam
as fast as they could toward the
shimmering piece of shell. But before
they or the goblins
could reach it,
a small pink
crab scuttled
over and
picked up the
shell piece in its pincers.

"That's definitely part of the golden
conch," Ally said in excitement, as
sparkles of light from the shell shone
through the water. "Come on!"

Before the fairies could get there,
however, the goblins reached the crab
first. One of them held out his hand.
"Give it here, Stalk-Eyes," he ordered
rudely.

The little crab held tightly to the shell, and some other, bigger crabs emerged from behind a rock to form a protective circle around their friend. They snapped the water with their pincers to keep the goblins away.

"How can we get rid of those goblins?" Rachel wondered, as one of them made a grab for the shell piece.

She turned to Ally. "Could Echo and the other dolphins chase them away? What do you think?"

Ally grinned. "You bet," she said, and whispered something to Echo. Echo nodded, her mouth falling open in a smile. She made a series of clicks and whistling sounds to the other dolphins.

Immediately, all the dolphins rushed toward the goblins, who looked absolutely terrified at the sight. "Don't eat me!" cried one. "Help! Swim for your life!"

"*Aaaarrrghh!*" yelled the other goblin.
"Mommy!"
The frightened goblins turned and
swam off as fast as they could. Rachel
giggled. She loved it when a plan
worked out!

"Now we just need to persuade the little crab to trade us," Ally said thoughtfully, picking up a small stone from the seabed. She waved her wand, and a stream of silvery light danced through the water and all around the stone. Ally's magic had turned it into a gleaming white pearl!

Ally swam over to the crab. "Look at this beautiful pearl," she said, holding it out to show him. "Would you like to trade it for that piece of broken shell?"

The crab immediately dropped the piece of golden conch shell and picked

up the pearl, looking very happy.

"Thank you." Kirsty smiled, reaching out to take the piece of shell.

"Look out!" Rachel shouted suddenly, as the goblins, followed by Echo and the other dolphins, shot back through the grotto. The goblins and dolphins were going so fast that they caused a current

of water to sweep through the cave.
The shell lifted right off the seabed and
surged away from the three fairies.

Kirsty lunged for it, but before she could grab the piece of shell, a goblin snatched it up and swam quickly out of the grotto.

"After him!" called Ally. "Don't let him get away!"

# Catch that Goblin!

Kirsty, Rachel, Ally, and Echo chased after the goblin. He swam all the way up to the surface. As the others followed, they suddenly heard a lot of noise. Once their heads broke the surface of the water, they discovered the source of all the racket.

"It's a water-skiing show!" Kirsty cried in alarm, swerving to avoid a speedboat as it roared past her. All around them speedboats zoomed along, towing water-skiers and wakeboarders behind them. Up on the beach, a crowd of spectators watched the action.

Just then, the girls saw one wakeboarder fly right past the goblin who was holding the piece of golden conch shell. He stretched out a hand and grabbed the piece of shell—and they realized that he was a goblin, too!

They watched in dismay as he zoomed away at an amazing speed. "We're never going to catch up with him," Rachel said. "There's no way we can swim that fast."

"No," said Ally, "but the dolphins can, can't they?" She grinned and leaped out of the water and onto Echo's back, taking hold of her back fin. Then she gave a whistle, and two other dolphins swam over to Kirsty and Rachel. "Ladies, your carriages await." Ally smiled. "Jump on board!"

Kirsty and Rachel didn't need to be told twice! They both flew out of the water and onto their own dolphins, clinging tightly to their fins. "And off we go," Ally cheered. "Come on, Echo!"

Echo and the two other dolphins surged through the sea, and Rachel almost fell off her dolphin's back in surprise. It was going so fast, she felt like she was flying!

A huge cheer went up as the spectators on the beach spotted the dolphins. The three fairies hunched low by the animals' fins, not wanting to be seen. The dolphins were closing in on the wakeboarding goblin. Suddenly, all three of them leaped out of the water at once, making the goblin jump in surprise.

The startled goblin lost his balance and tumbled into the sea, dropping the piece of the golden conch shell as he fell! "Oh, no!" he yelled in dismay, trying

to catch it. Echo was too quick for him, though. With another graceful leap into the air, she caught the piece of shell in her mouth and dove back into the water.

The other two dolphins that Kirsty and Rachel were riding on followed. Once they were all a safe distance from the goblins, the girls slipped off their backs.

"Thank you," Kirsty said, patting her dolphin's silver nose. "I enjoyed that so much."

Meanwhile, Ally was hugging Echo, delighted to have the piece of golden conch shell. "Good girl, Echo," she said happily. "And great job, Kirsty and Rachel! I'd better take Echo and this piece of shell back to the Fairyland Royal Aquarium now, but I'm sure we'll meet again. I'll change you two back into your human form first. Thanks for everything!"

Kirsty and Rachel hugged the smiling fairy and Echo, too. They would

never forget their wonderful dolphin
adventure!

Ally waved her wand and a stream of
silver sparkles surrounded them all, so
that everything seemed to blur before
their eyes. When the sparkly whirlwind
died down, the girls were back on the
beach at Lea-on-Sea, behind the very
same cluster of rocks where they'd
started their fairy adventure.

"We were only gone for a minute," Kirsty said as she looked up to check the time on the clock tower. Then she smiled at Rachel. "That was the most exciting minute of my life, I think!"

Rachel was smiling, too, as she gazed out at the waves tumbling onto the shore. "I can't wait for our next ocean adventure," she said. "I think this is going to be a very magical vacation!"

Ally the Dolphin Fairy has found
her piece of the golden conch shell!
Now Rachel and Kirsty must help . . .

# Amelie
### the Seal Fairy!

Join their next underwater adventure
in this special sneak peek. . . .

# Magic Lantern

"Look at the lighthouse, Rachel!" Kirsty
Tate exclaimed to her best friend, Rachel
Walker. "Isn't it beautiful?"

Rachel shaded her eyes from the sun
and gazed at the lighthouse. The tall,
newly-painted red and white building
stood proudly among the rocks at the
harbor entrance. "It's very nice," Rachel

agreed. "It looks so much better than it did before."

"Everyone in town helped raise the money to renovate the lighthouse and turn it into an artists' studio," Kirsty's gran explained. Kirsty and Rachel were spending their spring vacation with her in the coastal town of Leamouth. "There's been a lot of work going on since the last time you were here."

As they approached the lighthouse, they saw that a line of easels overlooking the ocean had been set up outside. There were people sitting at some of the easels, painting views of the water and the lighthouse. "Maybe you'd like to explore the lighthouse for a while, girls, while I'm at my painting class," Gran suggested as she headed for an empty easel. "It's been

renovated inside, too, and there are lots of paintings on display. Even the big old lantern right at the top is working again. It's just for show, though. Ships don't need it to tell them where the shore is anymore."

Leaving Gran to unpack her paints and brushes, the girls wandered over to the lighthouse. The door was open, and Rachel and Kirsty went inside.

"Let's climb right up to the top," Rachel suggested.

"Good idea," said Kirsty, heading for the narrow spiral staircase. The walls on either side of the steps were hung with watercolor paintings, pencil sketches, and collages of different views of Leamouth. The girls stopped occasionally to take closer looks.

"I can't believe the big lantern is

working again, can you?" Kirsty asked as they climbed higher. "Last time we were here, the bulb was broken and Shannon had to use her fairy magic to make it light up."

"Yes, we had to stop that cruise ship, the *Seafarer*, from hitting the rocks," Rachel remembered. "That was *almost* a disaster, thanks to Jack Frost and his goblins!" She glanced up the stairs as they approached the top of the lighthouse. "The lantern is probably only turned on at night—"

Suddenly Rachel broke off, her heart pounding. They were almost at the top of the stairs now and she could see a sparkling golden glow ahead of them, coming from the lantern room.

"What is it, Rachel?" Kirsty asked curiously from behind her.

"I can see a light coming from the lantern!" Rachel declared.

"Why would the lantern be turned on?" Kirsty asked, confused. "It's the middle of the day."

"That glow *isn't* from a lightbulb," Rachel replied, "I think it's fairy magic!"

Breathless with anticipation, the two girls ran up the last few steps and into the room at the very top of the lighthouse. Sure enough, the lantern was glowing with a magical golden light.

"Look, Rachel!" Kirsty cried, pointing at the mirrors surrounding the lantern. "There are lots of fairies!"

"But they all look the *same*," Rachel said, sounding confused. Then she burst out laughing. "Kirsty, it's only *one* fairy!" Rachel explained. "Those are just reflections."

The girls heard a tinkling little laugh, and a tiny fairy flitted out from inside the lantern. She had long brown hair with straight bangs, and she wore a patterned dress, gladiator sandals, and a chunky beaded bracelet on her wrist.

"It's me, girls," she cried, "Amelie the Seal Fairy!"

# RAINBOW magic™

# There's Magic in Every Series!

The Rainbow Fairies

The Weather Fairies

The Jewel Fairies

The Pet Fairies

The Fun Day Fairies

The Petal Fairies

The Dance Fairies

The Music Fairies

The Sports Fairies

The Party Fairies

## Read them all!

■ SCHOLASTIC

www.scholastic.com

www.rainbowmagiconline.com

HIT entertainment

RMFAIRY2

# SPECIAL EDITION

# Three Books in One—
# More Rainbow Magic Fun!

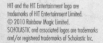

www.scholastic.com
www.rainbowmagiconline.com

HIT entertainment

RMSPECIAL